To Precious Girls everywhere who know that forgiveness is a beautiful way to show love to others. May you enjoy a lifetime of beautiful friendships!

Lost and Found

By Cindy Kenney
Illustrated by the Precious Moments Creative Studio

Library of Congress Control Number: 2009926767

Kenney, Cindy, *Lost and Found* / Cindy Kenney for Precious Moments, Inc.
Precious Moments # 990050 (Tradepaper)
                    # 990049 (Hardcover)

ISBN 978-0-9819885-2-8 (Tradepaper)
ISBN 978-0-9819885-3-5 (Hardcover)

Printed in China

Table of Contents

CHAPTER ONE
The Letter

I brought the mail in and saw it right away—a letter addressed to Mom and Dad: *Mr. and Mrs. Charles Bennett and The Precious Girls Club.*

Hmmm. Mom and Dad aren't members of The Precious Girls Club . . . but I am! I thought, reaching for the envelope.

When we first moved to Shine, Wisconsin, we started The Precious Girls Club so I could make friends, and we could all learn about the ways God made us special, then find fun ways to use our talents to help others. Since it started, our club has done a bunch of cool things!

I was just about to rip open the envelope when my dog, Patches, and my kitten, Sparky, started running circles around me. They love to play.

"What are you guys up to?"

"Ruff! Ruff!" Patches answered. Sparky purred and nuzzled against me. I reached over to pet them.

"Hey, you two, I've got something important to read. I may have won a trip somewhere!"

I stared at the sealed envelope. What if we didn't win a trip? Even though the President of the United States chose us as one of the groups to represent *Today's Students for a Better Tomorrow,* it didn't guarantee we'd win one of the trips. I put the envelope back on the table.

"What do you think, Patches? Mom and Dad will be home any minute. Maybe I should wait to hear the news from them. What should I do?"

"Ruff!"

"Right! I can't wait another minute!"

I grabbed the envelope and ripped it open just as my parents pulled into the driveway. I quickly scanned the first paragraph.

We are pleased to announce that we have

chosen The Precious Girls Club to receive an all-expense paid trip . . .

"We won! Oh, wow! We won, we won!"

I tossed the letter back on the table and ran outside to meet my parents.

"Guess what!" I shrieked. "We won a trip!"

"What?" Mom asked, handing me a bag of groceries to carry into the house.

"The Precious Girls Club won a trip for the *Today's Students for a Better Tomorrow* contest!"

"That's great, Katie!" Mom said, with a half-hug, trying not to crush the groceries between us. "Let's get these into the house and we can talk about it some more. Okay?"

"Yep!" I giggled, skipping back into the house.

Dad held the door as we brought stuff into the kitchen. Then he picked up the letter to read.

"Isn't it cool, Dad?"

"I think it's terrific, honey," he said. "But there is one problem."

"Oh no! What's wrong?" I asked. "Don't tell me it's a week we can't go!"

"This envelope isn't addressed to you, Katie."

"It sort of is," I objected.

"Hmmm. What part of Mr. and Mrs. Charles Bennett contains the name Katie?"

"Not that part, Dad, but I am one of the people on line two. I'm in The Precious Girls Club!"

"I'll tell you what," he said. "I'll forgive you, but I want you to respect other people's property. This letter is addressed to your mother and me, and you should have waited for us to open it."

"Yes, sir," I said. "I'm sorry."

"I don't want this to happen again, Katie. Is that understood?"

"It won't."

I watched as he continued to read. I may have opened the letter, but I hadn't read much. "What trip did we win, Dad? Where are we going?"

He folded the letter and slipped it back in the envelope. "I think it's only fair that you wait to find out when we tell the rest of the group tomorrow."

"Awwww! C'mon, Daddy. P-l-eeeeease," I begged.

"Sorry. Time for bed. It's a school night."

"Okay," I said and sulked off to my room.

CHAPTER TWO

Tripped Up

The clock moved painfully slow as I waited for school to end so we could rush to my house and finally hear where we'd be going. Everyone in the Precious Girls Club was bursting with excitement when I told them about winning a trip.

"My mom and dad go to those all-inclusive resorts," Jenny said. "I hope that's what we get."

"I don't even know what that is," Lidia admitted.

"I've always wanted to ride horses!" Nicola said. "In fact, I think one of the trips is a week at a Dude Ranch. Wouldn't that be so cool?"

"I read that one trip is to Europe! Can you imagine it? We might get to see the Eiffel Tower!"

"Another trip is a cruise. How awesome would that be?" Becca asked.

I frowned. "What if the boat sank?"

Everyone looked at me strangely. I just shrugged.

"Maybe we'll get the trip to Disneyland!" Lidia wondered.

"What if we get stuck with the backpacking trip?" Kirina asked.

"I feel sorry for that group," Avery laughed.

"I wouldn't go," Jenny groaned.

"I hope it's the ski trip to the mountains! I've always wanted to learn how to ski," Avery said.

Finally, the waiting was over as my parents stood in front of us and my mom said, "Okay girls, settle down. The letter says: *We are pleased to award the Precious Girls Club a full week's vacation to Pictured Rocks National Lakeshore!*"

"Wow! Isn't that in Europe?" Becca asked.

"I think I remember reading something about Pictured Rocks in Australia," Nicola said.

"Oh cool!" shrieked Avery as the rest of us "Oooed" and "Ahhhed."

"Whoa! Hold on, girls," Dad said. "Pictured Rocks is a place where Mrs. Bennett and I used to go years ago, before you were born."

"Where is it Dad?" I asked.

"It's a beautiful place in the Upper Peninsula of Michigan, along Lake Superior," he said.

"Really?" Becca asked, not nearly as excited.

"You girls will love it!" Mom added. "We'll get to spend seven wonderful days hiking along the lakeshore. The prize includes brand new hiking and camping gear for all of us! Isn't that wonderful?"

The room was silent. The news stunned us. We'd won the awful trip we had joked about during lunchtime.

"That's not very far," Bailey said at last.

"Only one state away," Kirina moaned.

"I've never even heard of it," Becca whined.

"Well, I'm not going! I wouldn't be caught dead living in filth for a week," Jenny complained.

"I can't believe this!" I grumbled.

"C'mon, girls," Aunt Ella chimed in as she brought in her special brownies. I guess they were our consolation prize. "Pictured Rocks is an amazing place. You'll swim and pick some delicious blueberries! Not to mention how much you'll value this grand place that God created."

"Whoop-de-doo! I'm still not going," Jenny said.

"You're missing the *big* picture," my Mom told us. "Let's be grateful for being chosen. Remember why you entered the contest in the first place?"

"You were chosen because you're a special group of girls," my dad added. "This is an honor and a special gift, yet all you can do is complain."

He was right. Still, we were disappointed about the great trips we had missed out on.

"My family goes camping all the time you guys! We have a terrific time. It's fun!" Lidia said.

Eventually, we talked about the fun stuff we'd do on the trip, but Jenny still refused to participate.

"Don't be so applethetic about this," I said, trying to be convincing.

"I think you mean *apathetic*, dear," Aunt Ella corrected as she and my parents went toward the kitchen to let us sort things out.

"Oh ya," I said, feeling my cheeks turn red. I like using new words, but sometimes I mix them up a little at first.

It took a while, but we finally started to get excited and began to make plans for the trip. It really was a generous gift. We were all going to get new hiking boots, jackets, backpacks, and tents.

"So that's it? You've all decided to go on this crummy trip?" Jenny asked.

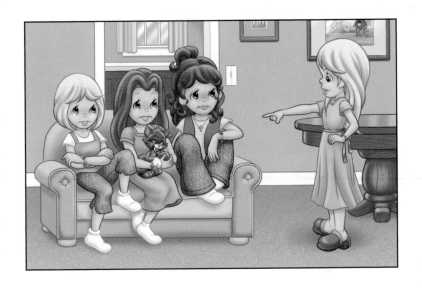

We nodded.

"It's all *her* fault!" Jenny pouted and pointed at me. "If it wasn't for you, no one would feel this way. You've taken all of my friends away!"

"But Jenny, *you're* my friend too," I said.

"No, I'm not. If *I* hadn't joined this club, the others wouldn't have either," Jenny whined and stormed out of the house.

"She's so stuck up," Avery sighed.

"She thinks she's better than everyone else. Don't worry, Katie. You didn't do anything wrong,"

Nicola offered.

"I'm glad she's not going," Becca said. "And I don't care if she quits the club."

Hearing the ruckus, my mom came in and stopped us from going any further. She tried to explain things from Jenny's point of view, but she wasn't very convincing. "I hope you can remember that it's a privilege to be part of a terrific group like this with such a special mission," she said.

"What about Jenny?" asked Avery. "Doesn't she have to remember that too?"

"Of course, but no one is perfect. We all have faults and flaws. That's why it's important to treat one another with grace and forgiveness. In anger Jenny said some things she didn't mean."

"I think she meant them," Kirina huffed.

"So what are we going to do?" asked Lidia.

"I say let's go without her," Avery pouted.

"I think we should convince her to come with us," I said.

We were in a real pickle.

CHAPTER THREE

Getting a Check-Up

"Are you mad at me, Faith?" I asked my best friend and guardian angel.

When we moved to Shine, Wisconsin, I was super sad about moving. My Dad gave my sister Anna and me two beautiful snow globes. Inside, danced two pretty angels, Hope and Faith. One day, I was feeling especially miserable and Faith sprang to life right before my eyes! I couldn't believe it, but it actually happened! She whooshed around in a sparkle of shiny colors, making me laugh and forget about my problems.

Whenever I get in a pickle or need somebody to talk to, Faith is always there. She helps me when I get confused or don't know what to do about something. But there is a catch. No one else can see or hear her! I guess that's okay. I'm just really glad she's my friend. I love her a whole bunch.

Faith had been acting strangely ever since we won the trip to Pictured Rocks, but I didn't know why.

"Why do you think I'm mad at you, Munchkin?" she asked zipping over to my desk and landing on my math homework.

"You haven't been acting the same this week. I thought maybe I did something to make you mad. Did I?"

"Nope."

She zoomed back into the air, spun around the room a few times, and went back to the window where she perched herself comfortably on the sill.

"See! You just did it again," I said, getting up to walk over to her. "It's the way you're talking to me—or not talking to me."

Faith turned toward me and smiled. "Maybe it's the way *you're* talking to *me* . . . and others."

I was confused! I wasn't sure what she meant. "I don't understand. The way *I'm* talking to *you*? Ohhhh!"

I said aloud as it started sinking in. "You mean that *I've* been the one acting weird lately, right?"

I could tell by the way she grinned and looked back at me that I was onto something.

I had been really angry with Jenny . . . but I also had every right to be after what she said to me!

"What you need is a check-up, Munchkin," Faith said. "You need to stop and think about how you've been acting ever since you won that trip. Then think about what God wants you to do. Do you remember the purpose for starting the Precious Girls Club?"

"Sure I do—to bring us all together so we could make friends and use the talents God gave us to have fun doing things for others."

"Maybe you've been so caught up in your frustration with Jenny that you let it take over everything else," she suggested.

"Yep, I guess. God probably doesn't want me to act like that, does He?"

"You tell me," she winked. "I think you know."

"Oh Faith, I know we should be thankful for winning such a great prize. If we hadn't heard about those other trips, we'd have been jumping up and down, thrilled about winning. Instead, we've been jealous of the others who got the better trips."

"How do you know they're going to be better? You haven't even given your trip a chance," Faith said as she fluttered over to kiss me on the cheek.

"I guess you're right. My mom and dad really liked it there. But Jenny's causing a bunch of trouble because she won't go with us."

"Haven't you ever made a comment in anger

and refused to do something?

"Yep, I guess. I refused to help my parents at the food pantry last year because I wanted to do an overnight with my friends. After I did the work, I learned a lot about the people who need help. Plus I felt really good that I had helped."

"How come you went, even after you refused to go?" Faith asked.

"Because my parents forgave me for acting badly and gave me another chance . . . just like we should do for Jenny!"

"You're a pretty smart kid, you know," Faith winked. She gave me a hug and pointed at my math book. "Better get back to work."

After talking to Faith, I felt a lot better about things. I even started to feel good about the backpacking trip. Of course, how to forgive Jenny and convince her to come on the trip was another problem altogether.

CHAPTER FOUR
Picture This

At first, I thought dealing with Jenny would be impossible, so I said a prayer and asked God to help me forgive her. I tried hard, even though she made it super difficult.

Faith helped me remember how God wants us to treat others. "If in doubt, just think about what you would do if God was actually walking right beside you. How would you feel about your choices then?"

"Everyone would be different if that happened!" I said.

"Exactly!" Faith agreed. "Katie, just remember that even though you can't see God, He is always with you, and that's how you should live every day."

Even though Jenny told us to go without her, we persuaded her to come with us. We told her how much we would miss her, and she finally agreed.

"Jenny is a good leader, and she can be pretty funny sometimes," I said to Faith later. "She has a lot of good qualities."

"I'm proud of you, Munchkin. You're focusing on others and how you can help them. I know it's not always easy."

"You can say that again!"

As we stood by the Pictured Rocks ranger station waiting for my dad to get our camping permit, Jenny started complaining. "These hiking boots are so bulky!" she griped. "I couldn't bring anything I wanted, not even my nail polish!"

"If I can do this, so can you darlin'!" Aunt Ella said. She was looking forward to seeing the place where my mom and dad made so many memories.

"Woof!" said Moses, Aunt Ella's big black and yellow dog that had once saved me when I fell through the ice.

"Ruff, ruff!" Patches echoed his buddy.

We spent the first night in the Pictured Rocks Lodge getting ready for our six-night hiking trip. After dinner, we gathered in a big room. We all held hands as my mom prayed, "Heavenly Father, we ask you to be with us this week. Help us to discover fun and new experiences. Show us how to be good friends. Thank you for this amazing opportunity to enjoy this incredible world you created. God, please keep us safe. Amen."

"Okay, everybody, now we're going to do something very important," my dad said. "We're going to cook up some delicious treats so we won't starve this week!"

Everybody cheered. My dad was always involved in anything concerning food, especially eating! So he showed us how to prepare food for our trip.

We made dried banana chips by slicing up bananas and drying them in the oven, bags of trail mix, tons of energy bars, and we even prepared

biscuit mix to use later in the trip.

Aunt Ella gave each of us craft and game supplies to carry in our backpacks, "In case it rains and we get stuck in our tents."

"In case it rains?" Jenny moaned. You mean it might rain while we're out there?"

"It's hard to control the weather, dear, but the forecast for this week looks nice," Aunt Ella said.

"How can we possibly survive in the rain? That means we'll get all *wet*!" Jenny howled.

"Hey, Jen. They don't have escalators to get you up the hills, either," Nicola laughed.

"And there aren't any McDonalds or a hair salon along the way," Becca giggled.

Finally, Jenny laughed too. Then my dad gave us some safety tips. "Girls, pay attention. This stuff is important," my dad said, then waited until the giggling and whispers died down.

"Dress in layers so you can take a layer off or put one on if it gets too hot or cold. Keep your rain poncho handy in case it rains. Wear sunscreen and a hat for sun protection. Take care of your feet. First, put on the thin socks I gave you. Then put the wool socks over them whenever you're hiking. Bring at least two bandanas. You can use them as a washcloth, a towel, a sweatband, or even as a small packsack."

By bedtime, we were as ready as we could be. I was the last one to leave the room with my backpack. As I turned out the light, Faith sprang out of a pocket with a sparkle of color.

"Faith, I didn't know you were here!"

"I'm always with you, Munchkin!"

"Oh good! Otherwise, I'd miss you way too much!" I said. "I sure hope this trip goes well."

"You'll have a terrific time. Just remember what I said. Hike those trails as if God was right beside you the entire way, and don't you worry, God *is* always with you! Sleep tight, kiddo."

"I will," I answered and snuggled into bed. "Goodnight, God! I hope you sleep well before our big trip too." If God was going to be walking along side me, He would need His rest just like me!

CHAPTER FIVE
Are We There Yet?

"Hi ho! Hi ho! It's off to the woods we go!" we sang that first morning as we marched along the trail.

We were off to a good start. My parents were right about how beautiful it was. The waves of Lake Superior crashed into pretty, brightly colored rocks sparkling in the sunshine along the trail. The water stretched as far as you could see!

"I'm tired!" whined Jenny. "When do we get to take a break? My feet hurt. I don't think I can walk another step. *Pleeeeeease* let's take a break!"

"Okay, everybody, let's take five," my dad said as he stopped and took off his backpack.

We all did the same, then reached for our water bottles and trail mix.

Aunt Ella poured water into a bowl for Moses and Patches who eagerly lapped it up.

"Finally!" Jenny sighed. "I'm exhausted. Can we camp here tonight?"

"Trust me, our campsite will be a lot nicer than this," my dad told her.

"We must have walked fifty miles by now!"

"Nope, just a little over a mile," my mom smiled looking at her map.

We were all a little surprised to hear that.

"Don't forget that we're going up and down a great deal. It's not like walking along a sidewalk," she reminded us.

"How much farther?" Jenny asked.

"A few more hours. The time will go by fast, you'll see," my mom answered.

Jenny groaned. That's pretty much how the day went. The rest of us told stories, jokes, and played games along the way. Jenny continued to whine, "Are we there yet?"

"We're all tired, so just chill out!" Nicola ordered.

"Stop whining! You're going to make this trip miserable for everybody," Becca said.

Then my mom announced, "We're here! This is our campsite for the next couple days."

It was super beautiful. We were high on a bluff overlooking the lake. A beautiful stream ran along one side of the campground and a soft, sandy beach was nestled in a small cove by the water.

Everyone worked together setting up camp. Things were going well, until . . .

"I have to go to the bathroom," Jenny said. "Mrs. Bennett, would you point the way?"

"Don't you remember what we discussed last night at our meeting?" my mom said.

"Jenny was still in the shower," Avery giggled.

"What are you talking about?" Jenny asked.

"We passed the last outhouse at our last rest stop, Jenny," my dad said.

"That was two hours ago!"

"Yep, that's about right."

"Then what am I supposed to do?"

We all listened as my dad explained what to do in the great outdoors when an outhouse wasn't available.

"Ewww! That's . . . that's disgusting!" Jenny shrieked. "I won't do it!"

"Suit yourself," my dad said. "But if you do go, remember to use the buddy system. No one ever leaves camp without a partner."

"We know!" the girls answered.

Mom told us we must never bring food or anything scented into our tents. Otherwise, we could get an unpleasant visit from an unwanted critter. Dad showed us how to hang our food high between two trees so animals couldn't get into it.

Cooking over a campfire was fun. We carefully mixed water with the homemade biscuit mix we'd prepared before starting our hike. Some of the girls mixed up stew while others prepared an area for eating. The food tasted so good!

After we did dishes, we gathered on the beach to watch the sunset. My parents made a campfire and we sang songs, told jokes, and toasted marshmallows.

"Knock, knock," Kirina began.

"Who's there?" we all shouted.

"Amos."

"Amos who?"

"A-mos-quito just bit me!"

Everyone roared with laughter.

"Look at all those stars!" I said, gazing at the night sky. I'd never seen so many stars! It was awesome! I smiled. I knew God was right there with us, just as Faith said He would be. Not only that, but He had created all of it! I'll never forget the way I felt that night.

Just then, there was a crunching sound coming from our campsite.

"What's that?" asked Lidia, startled.

"It's coming from the tents!" cried Nicola.

"Sounds sofishus!" I announced.

"Huh?"

"You know, sofishus! When you think somebody might be up to something fishy."

"Oh! You mean *suspicious*," my mom said.

"Uh, yeah. That's what I mean—suspicious."

"Don't worry," my dad said, already on his feet, heading up toward the tents. We all followed.

"It's behind my tent!" Becca howled.

"No! I think he's over there!" yelled Lidia.

When my dad's flashlight beam hit one of the tents, a raccoon waddled out, eating a candy bar. Dad and the dogs chased it, making certain that it wouldn't bother us again. He returned to the campsite holding several scraps of a torn candy bar wrapper.

We were all suddenly silent. Even Moses and Patches quietly lay by our feet.

"Didn't we specifically tell you *'no food'* in the tents? That means gum, candy, mints, *everything!*"

No one said anything.

"Who does this belong to?" he asked, while looking at the hole in the tent where the raccoon had gone in to get the yummy treat.

"That's Jenny, Becca, and Kirina's tent."

All three girls looked surprised, and that made my dad angry. "You're lucky it was just a raccoon and not a bear."

"A bear!" Jenny screamed.

"Honey, don't scare them," my mom cautioned.

"Let's make this a trip we can all enjoy, okay?" my dad said. "Don't let this happen again."

He quietly walked away. Lesson learned, or so I thought. I sure got the message loud and clear!

"You don't have to worry about animals if you follow the rules," my mom said gently. "It's been a long day. Let's call it a night, shall we? Jenny, Kirina, and Becca, grab your things and wiggle into other tents for tonight. Mr. Bennett and I will repair your tent tomorrow. Goodnight, girls."

After my mom disappeared, Jenny said, "Geez, it was just a candy bar! Stupid raccoon."

"Stupid *raccoon?*" Becca bellowed. "Who put the candy in the tent, Jenny? Thanks to you, we all have to be squished tonight!"

And squished we were.

CHAPTER SIX

Tug of War

There was something about this place that made me feel different. Maybe it was the fresh air and maybe it was because every place we went had something beautiful to see. Maybe it was because the people who were most important to me were all here together in one place. Or, maybe it was knowing that God was really here with me.

Jenny was glad it was a free day, but that didn't mean there was nothing to do. It seemed like there wasn't enough time in the day to do all the cool stuff we had planned!

Aunt Ella showed us how to make some super cool stick rafts. We were going to work on them all week and then race them down the stream the day before we went home.

We swam and picked the biggest, juiciest sweetest blueberries I'd ever tasted! Most of us had bellyaches from eating too many even before we brought them back to camp. Then we tried to play tug of war, but that ended when no one wanted to be on Jenny's team. It was awkward.

"Look! That cloud looks like an elephant!" I said, pointing to the sky as we lay on the beach.

"That one looks like a turtle!" Kirina laughed.

"Where? Oh ya, I see it," Avery said.

"Anyone know what kind of clouds those are?" my mom asked.

"Accumulating clouds!" I said, remembering her talk about them before.

"You're close, honey," Mom said. "They're called cumulus clouds. They look like big puffy cotton balls. Understanding clouds can be helpful when you're backpacking."

"How come?" Lidia asked.

"The smaller the clouds, the less chance of rain," Mom continued. "The bigger and darker they get, the more likely it will rain or even hail. The longer it takes for clouds to turn dark, the longer the storm will last."

"What about those long thin clouds?"

"Ahh, those are cirrostratus clouds. There are also altocumulus clouds that are smaller ones that come in rows, parallel to each other. Those usually mean rain in twenty-four hours or less."

"Looks like tomorrow will be another nice day then," Bailey said.

"Except that we have to hike again," Jenny complained.

"Tomorrow we will see some of the most spectacular rocks you can imagine!" Mom said.

I could tell she was excited about it, but Jenny started to grumble. One by one, we all left the beach until Jenny was alone. She was scowling when she came up to the tents a little later. "Thanks for telling me you all came back up here."

The girls looked at her briefly, then turned around to hear the rest of the story I was telling.

"See!" Jenny wailed, pointing at me. "*Katie's* the problem! It never used to be like this until she moved here! Katie Bennett, you've ruined my life!" Jenny stomped her foot, turned toward a trail, and headed into the woods.

"Jenny!" my mom called. "No one goes off without a buddy!"

Jenny growled and disappeared into her tent. Later, after she had time to cool down, my mom went to talk to her. I was resting in the next tent and heard most of what they said.

"My friends don't like me anymore!" Jenny sniffed. It sounded as if she had been crying.

"I don't think that's true, Jenny," my mom said.

"When I show up, they leave. When I have an idea, they ignore me. When I talk, they don't listen! I know Katie is your daughter, but things were never like this until she came along."

"Maybe this has nothing to do with Katie or your other friends. Maybe things are happening the way they are because of you, Jenny."

"Huh?"

"Sometimes it's a good idea to stop and give some thought to what you may be doing to make the people around you act the way they do. It could be that you are doing or saying things that are pushing them away."

Jenny was surprised. "I'm not trying to push them away!"

"I know, sweetie," my mom said softly, "but instead of blaming others, it might help to think how you can change to make things different."

At first, I thought Jenny understood what my mom was saying. She thanked her, and they hugged. But after my mom left, I heard Jenny mumble, "Nobody understands! If I'm going to be miserable and not have any fun on this trip, everybody else can be miserable too!"

Uh oh, I thought. *What did she mean by that?*

CHAPTER SEVEN

Pinecones and Needles and Ants!

"Hey, you guys, look!" Nicola said. "There's a fork in the road!"

"You know what that means don't you?" Mom asked. "It must be time to eat!"

Everybody laughed. Our hike to the next campsite was going well. Jenny was still griping about everything from blisters on her feet to mosquito bites. She wanted to take a break every ten minutes. My dad got so tired of it he carried her backpack, hoping she'd stop complaining. It didn't work.

"Why don't grizzly bears wear shoes?" asked Nicola.

"I know this one," Becca laughed, "because

they like walking around in *bear* feet!"

"What if we actually came across a bear in the woods?" Kirina asked. "How do we outrun it?"

"We don't have to outrun it. We just have to outrun you!" Avery said, causing lots of giggles.

When we got to our new campsite, setting up was easier. We knew what to do and worked hard, realizing that the sooner we finished, the more time we had to do fun stuff. Even Jenny was being cooperative. It was nice not hearing her complain.

"Who wants to help me start the dinner fire?" my mom asked.

She had plenty of volunteers. Everybody liked working around the campfire. "Does anyone see my matches?" Mom asked.

"I do!" Lidia said. She grabbed them from the table and told us a funny story. "The first time my grandparents took us camping, we had a problem lighting the fire. Gramps told my gram that he couldn't light the fire with the matches she'd brought. Gram said, "I don't understand. I tried everything out before we left home, just like you asked me to!"

We all cracked up laughing. Mom offered to cook dinner while Dad and Aunt Ella showed us how to create a wilderness miniature golf course. We played using sticks for clubs and pinecones for balls. It was hilarious!

It wasn't until we ate that we realized Jenny hadn't been with us for any of the fun. Just then, she wandered up to the campfire.

"Where have you been?" Becca asked.

"Resting. I have blisters, you know," she pouted.

"Believe me, we know!" Avery answered.

After dinner, Jenny disappeared again, claiming she was tired. No one minded.

By the time we finally went to bed, I couldn't wait to snuggle into my warm, cozy sleeping bag.

"Ouch!" I yelped. Instead of the fuzzy warmth I'd expected, I pushed my feet into a pile of prickly pine needles and pinecones! Nicola groaned as she discovered the same thing in her bag. It wasn't easy to get rid of them. Many had dug their way into the cushiony part of the bag and had to be picked out one by one.

We knew who was responsible. There was only one person who both wanted to do something like this and had the time to do it.

While we were picking needles out of our bags, we heard Bailey scream. "A snake! There's a snake inside my bag!"

Bailey, Avery, and Lidia came running out of their tent at the same time my parents appeared.

"What's going on out here?"

"There's a snake in our tent!" yelled Avery.

My dad bravely went inside the tent to check it out. He came out a second later holding up an air mattress with a leak making a hissing sound.

"Sorry, Mr. Bennett."

"What are you three girls doing out here with your sleeping bags?" he asked.

"There are pine needles inside our bags, Dad."

"Honey, I told you to clean your shoes or just take them off before you go into the tent. Now please go back to bed and get some sleep."

He blew me a kiss and Mom gave me a hug.

At least Kirina and Becca didn't have to worry. They were in Jenny's tent, so they were safe. I did my best to be forgiving. I remembered that God was right there with me watching and listening. Who knows, maybe He was picking pine needles out of His sleeping bag too!

The next morning, Becca and Kirina came hopping out of their tent barefoot, looking as if they had the heebee jeebies.

"What's wrong?" Nicola asked.

"Jenny put food inside our hiking boots and set them outside the tent. There are gazillions of ants crawling in them!"

I guess they weren't off the hook after all.

The next two days were filled with tricks and pranks. A line of clean, dry clothes "accidentally" fell into a pile of mud. Jenny somehow "forgot" to hang up our trail mix, so we came back from the beach one afternoon and found chipmunks, squirrels, and birds enjoying a Thanksgiving feast.

Jenny smiled as we got the food bag down for dinner. "Oh look! My trail mix got put away! Mmm! I just love this stuff!"

I went inside my tent to write down some of my favorite memories from the trip. All of a sudden, something bumpy moved in my sleeping bag. Jenny was at it again, and I was mad. I grabbed my hiking boot and prepared to pounce on whatever crawled out.

"Yikes!" Faith shouted as I lifted my boot and started to swing. She sprang into the air a second before my boot landed on the bag.

"Faith! Are you okay?" I asked.

"I guess so. What was that for?"

"Jenny has been doing pranks. I thought she put something in my bag, but it was you. She is going to ruin our trip if she keeps it up."

"You remember what we talked about before the trip, don't you?"

"Of course, Faith, but Jenny makes it hard to keep on forgiving her!"

"Aren't you glad God doesn't put a limit on how much He'll forgive you?"

"Yes, but I thought we're supposed to learn from our mistakes."

"Some people take a little longer than others," she said with a yawn. "Sorry, I just woke up. It was nice and cozy down there."

"Mom tried to talk to Jenny, but I think it made things worse."

"Remember the story of Joseph in the Bible? Joseph's brothers were jealous of him. They were so mean that they tossed him in a well; sold him as a slave; and lied to their father about it! When he worked as a slave, his master's wife lied about him and he was sent to jail! But Joseph knew that God was always with him. He kept loving and obeying God the whole time."

"And God took care of him?"

"That's right, Munchkin. Things worked out real well for Joe. When his brothers came to him for help years later, he forgave them for everything, just like God keeps forgiving us."

"And that's what God wants us to do," I said. "I get it."

"Katie!" my friends were calling.

"I gotta go, Faith. Thanks for the talk."

"Anytime, Munchkin," she smiled, snuggling into the poufy softness of my pillow.

The girls were showing my mom the formation of clouds that had been building in the sky all day.

"Good observations!" my mom said. "We're in for a storm. Make sure you buckle everything down tight . . . and keep your ponchos handy.

The winds began blowing as we sat around the

campfire. Jenny chose to join us, but no one sat by her. Becca and Kirina quietly made plans to sleep in other tents. They were tired of sharing a tent with her.

Eventually, we all headed to bed. Jenny and I realized we were the last to leave. That meant it was our job to put out the fire. As we scooped up some water and poured it over the hot coals, I finally said, "I'm sorry you're not having much fun on our trip, Jenny." Immediately, I regretted opening my mouth.

"You should be sorry! All of this is your fault. I hate camping, Katie Bennett. I hate backpacking and hiking, and I hate this trip! I wish I'd never let you talk me into coming!" Jenny stomped off.

I had to admit that I was happy knowing she would be all alone in her tent tonight!

CHAPTER EIGHT

The Storm

The winds howled around our tents as the thunder rolled in. It began to rain. Each drop of rain sounded as if it would punch right through the canvas. Lightning flashed, causing the inside of our tents to brighten up before going dark again.

"Pssst, Katie! If lightning hits one of the trees above us, will it travel through the ground and electrocute us?" Nicola asked.

"I don't know," I said, pulling my sleeping bag closer around me. It was a cold night.

"What if our tent starts to leak?"

"It won't," I told her. "My dad said these are excellent tents, plus he waterproofed them too."

The storm seemed to last forever. I said a prayer, asking God to keep watch over us, just in

case He'd decided to bunk up in heaven tonight where I'm sure it was much more comfortable.

In the morning, the sun was shining and everything smelled wonderful! We were all a bit sleepier than usual, but our tents were dry inside.

"Our trip is almost over!" Nicola said as most of us ate breakfast.

"I don't want it to end," Avery moaned.

"Neither do I," said Lidia. "This week went by too fast!"

"Not for Jenny," I said.

"Speaking of . . . where is Jenny?" Mom asked.

"Still sleeping," Becca answered. "I haven't seen her yet this morning."

"Maybe the extra sleep will do her good," my dad said.

"True, but the girls should get her up if we're going to hike to Rainbow Falls and be back in time for the raft race," my mom yawned and stretched.

"I'll wake her!" Kirina offered.

"What kind of mood is she in today?" Nicola asked when Kirina returned.

"Who knows? She wasn't there."

Dad started grumbling about how Jenny never paid attention to the buddy system. By the time we finished our breakfast, she still hadn't shown up.

Suddenly, Becca came running from her tent, "Jenny's backpack and sleeping bag are gone! I think she ran away!"

CHAPTER NINE
Missing!

My parents ran to her tent. Jenny wasn't just missing. She was gone! They whispered something to each other and dashed off in opposite directions. Aunt Ella corralled the rest of us near our eating area.

"Who is Jenny's buddy?" Aunt Ella asked.

"I am!" Becca admitted. "But we haven't been very good buddies this week. She never wanted to go with me, so I just started asking someone else."

Nobody knew anything. Jenny hadn't said a word. We all felt terrible. Then Becca and Kirina admitted they hadn't slept in the tent with her.

"I yelled at her yesterday," Nicola admitted. "I wasn't very nice."

"I teased her about her hair all day long," Lidia confessed.

All I could think of is how much pleasure I had taken in knowing that she would be all alone in her tent last night. If I had told my parents, this would never have happened.

Aunt Ella looked at all of us with a great deal of disappointment. My parents returned looking nervous and worried. They talked with Aunt Ella then called us together.

"We're going to split into three search groups," Mom said. "Each group will go in a different direction, search for two hours, rest, and then turn back if she hasn't been found."

If *none* of the groups found her, my dad would hike out to the ranger's station to get help fast. We prepared our daypacks with water, food, and supplies.

"Do you think she was out in that terrible storm all night?" Lidia asked.

"No way. Jenny hates getting wet," Nicola answered.

"But what if she left *before* the storm began?"

The question hung in the air. No one wanted to answer it as each group silently took off down the trail, hoping to find Jenny soon.

CHAPTER TEN

Rainbow Falls

I was in my mom's group with Nicola, Moses, and Patches.

"C'mon boy," I whispered to Moses. "You helped save me, now help us find Jenny."

We went in the direction of Rainbow Falls, where we had planned to hike before this happened.

"I can't believe she didn't come back the minute the first raindrop fell," Nicola said. "She hates the rain!"

We thought about what it might have been like out in the woods during the storm. We each agreed it would have been very scary.

"What's that noise?" I asked.

"It sounds like the falls," said Mom. "Rainbow Falls should be right around the bend."

Moses led the way as we made our way closer to the sound of running water.

"Wow! It's gorgeous!" said Nicola.

Rainbow Falls was running faster than usual after the rain. The water fell down from a high bluff, splashing into the stream below. As the stream passed in front of the Pictured Rocks, you could see a rainbow of color sparking through the water.

"I wish everyone could see this," Nicola said.

"Yes, well, we must push on for a bit more," my mom urged.

"Maybe seeing Rainbow Falls is a sign of God's promise that He's watching over Jenny!" I said.

"Could be, honey," Mom agreed.

A quarter of a mile further, just as we were about to turn back, I heard a strange sound.

"What is that?"

"Woof, woof!" Moses heard it too.

"Ruff, ruff!" Patches added.

"It's probably just the falls again," Mom said.

We listened carefully, but heard nothing. Suddenly, Moses and Patches started barking louder. My mom was worried it was an animal. We all got real quiet. Then we heard a soft whimpering coming from the right side of the trail.

"Jenny!" we all called out at once.

Moses led the way as the sound of someone crying grew louder.

"Jenny! Please come out! We aren't angry with you!" my mom called.

It was difficult to hear with Rainbow Falls roaring nearby. As Moses sniffed around, I suddenly caught sight of Faith hovering above a large, rocky area. She waved me over, and I heard the sound get louder the closer I got!

"Where could she be?" my mom said.

Moses, Patches, and I hurried to the place where Faith hovered. She led us around the rocks. I bent over to peer beneath a small ledge covering a tiny, cave-like area.

"Oh no! Jenny, what happened to you?"

CHAPTER ELEVEN

A Little Help from a Friend

I crawled down and crouched over to hug Jenny. She was soaking wet and bleeding.

"Oh goodness, what happened? Katie, honey, let me get in there to see what happened," said my mom.

"She's shaking and won't let go of me," I whispered. "I don't know if she's okay, Mom!"

"Jenny, you're safe now," my mom said softly. "Please come out with Katie. Okay, honey?"

"Everyone is looking for you. We were so worried!" I said gently as I continued to hug her shivering body.

"C'mon, sweetheart," my mom urged. "We need to get you out of here and get you some help."

"Jenny, we really are your friends, no matter what. You have to believe me. We were scared to death when we discovered you were gone!" I said.

Slowly, Jenny let me help her out of the little cave. She looked so scared and frail. "I c-can't believe you really came to l-look for m-me!" she said.

Jenny told us how she tried to find her way back in the terrible storm. She'd left shortly before the storm began, convinced that she could find

the ranger's station before things got bad. Once it started raining, it got harder to see. The trails became muddy and slippery. She fell down a small, hilly area, filled with rocks and hurt her leg.

As Jenny talked, my mom took out her first aid kit and went to work on her leg. Jenny was very brave and let her do whatever needed to stop the bleeding. After my mom made a makeshift splint and bandaged up Jenny's leg, we quickly gathered some long, strong sticks to create a mat on which to carry Jenny back to camp.

We did our best to get her wet clothes off and replace them with dry, warm clothes we'd brought along. We put a jacket under her head. We tried to carry the mat, but in some places, we had to pull it behind us. It was slow going and difficult. The path went up and down and wound around curves. Slowly, we made our way back toward camp.

"I'm so sorry, Jenny. I never meant to cause you pain," I said, trying to apologize. But Jenny had become very quiet. I wasn't sure if she was hurt more than we realized or if she was too angry to speak.

Suddenly, we heard my dad calling. We were so relieved to see him, Becca, and Kirina heading down the trail toward us. When we hadn't returned on time, they had come to find us. With their extra help, we were able to get back to camp much faster.

When we arrived, everyone was thrilled to see Jenny. My dad repacked his daypack, told us to be careful, and took off right away for the ranger station to get help.

I returned to Jenny's side where everyone stood close, assuring her that she had been missed.

"Jenny, please forgive us. We're so thankful to have you as a friend. We all handled things very badly. I'm so sorry," I said.

I waited for her to respond, but instead of saying anything, Jenny's eyes closed and wouldn't open again.

"Mom!" I yelled. "Something's wrong!"

CHAPTER TWELVE
The Power of Forgiveness

My mom and Aunt Ella rushed over to Jenny as the girls parted to let them near. They shook her hard and her eyelids fluttered open.

"She's just fallen asleep after her long, terrifying night in the woods," my mom said.

"Jenny! Don't scare us like that!" I yelled.

Jenny gave me a big, sleepy smile and said, "That's more like it. That sounds more like the Katie I know."

Everyone laughed, including Jenny.

"How are you feeling?" my mom asked as I saw Faith flutter above Jenny's head, checking on her too.

"I'm a lot better now. Thanks for coming to get me. I'm really sorry for running away, Mrs.

Bennett. I'm sorry about a lot of things."

"What do you mean?" I asked.

"I mean that you and I are usually fighting about something." Jenny answered.

"Let's not worry about that now, okay?" my mom said.

"I was so angry, but now I realize that I was just being selfish and thinking only about myself. I hope all of you can forgive me."

"We do," everyone said together.

"I'll never forget last night. After I fell, I thought I was going to die. I could hardly move. The thunder and lightning flashed all around me in the pouring rain."

"How did you get in that little cave?" I asked.

"I don't really know. I guess I crawled there, but I don't know how I could have. I remember praying to God and telling Him how sorry I was. I was so mad about not getting my way. With each flash of lightning and boom of thunder, the whole week came crashing around me—all of the fun, games, songs, and stories. The cooking we did, the games we played, even our hikes, and how much we laughed! All I could think of was how I tried to mess it up for everyone. But instead of causing trouble for you, I just brought it all on myself."

"Okay darlin', we don't have to go through all of that now," Aunt Ella said.

"It's okay. I need to tell everyone that I realize what I've done. Last night, I told God I was sorry about everything. I begged Him to give me another chance. The next thing I remember, I was in that little cave."

"Maybe you had a guardian angel watching over you," I said, smiling at Faith. She did a little pirouette and curtsied. I somehow knew she had helped!

"Maybe I did," Jenny smiled. "Anyway, I'm so sorry that I ruined your vacation."

"You didn't," I said. "We all learned a lot on this trip—like, friends stick together forever, no matter what!"

In that moment, we all knew how important this trip had been for each of us. We had each learned so much, and we had grown in friendship, faith, and forgiveness.

Jenny dozed off while the rest of us took down the tents and got ready to go home. As we packed, Nicola discovered the raft she'd made that we were supposed to race tonight after dinner.

"Why don't you race them right now?" Aunt Ella said.

Jenny was awake and was leaning on her elbows. "Yes, race them now. Don't let me ruin everything. Just carry me over where I can watch!"

Everyone agreed. We brought Jenny down by the stream at the finish line, then ran up to the starting point and put our rafts in the stream.

Then Aunt Ella said, "On your mark, get set, go!"

CHAPTER THIRTEEN
The Race Is On!

The rafts bobbed up and down on the gentle current as they slowly made their way downstream. Everyone shouted words of encouragement, as if each little raft had a driver trying to weave her craft along the course.

We laughed hysterically as our rafts bumped into one another, tipped, flipped, and popped back up again.

One of the rafts sank. Another got stuck behind a big rock. Two of them collided and fell apart. None of them made it to the finish line. There weren't any winners or losers today—just friends who enjoyed a great time together.

The sound of a siren echoed through the otherwise peaceful woods, as several jeeps and an ambulance made their way down a nearby emergency road. They carefully loaded Jenny into the ambulance. Mom volunteered to go with her.

"Wait!" Jenny said. "Can Katie come too?"

Mom and Dad looked at me and said, "It's up to you."

I nodded and climbed in as the rest of the group loaded up the other jeeps, and we all headed for home.

• • •

A couple days later, I entered Jenny's hospital room. "Are you up for a visitor?"

"Sure! C'mon in!" Jenny answered and sat up higher in her bed.

"I brought you a special gift," I told her and took out a big box wrapped with a beautiful bow.

"What a pretty package!" she said, eager to unwrap it. She tore through the paper and lifted a musical snow globe from the box. A beautiful angel danced around inside. "Oh wow!"

"Her name is Grace which means to show mercy and forgiveness. I thought she would be a special reminder of our week together. I also thought you might like to have a guardian angel around even when you're not stuck in the middle of a forest in a huge thunderstorm! I hope she'll help to remind you that you're very special to all of us—no matter what."

"Even when I'm a pain to be around?" Jenny asked and laughed.

"Even then," I giggled.

"Thanks Katie. I really love it. This gift means a lot to me. I'm really glad we're friends!"

"Me too!" I said.

"Knock, knock! Can we come in?" my mom

asked, leading the way for the rest of The Precious Girls Club, my dad, and Aunt Ella.

"We got special permission to come in here all at once!" Nicola says. "Maybe it's because we did that puppet show for all the kids who were here last year."

Jenny grinned from ear to ear, happy to see everyone.

My mom told us she had a new charm she wanted to give us. We all held up our wrists and jingled the charms we had already collected on our bracelets.

"This charm is very special, particularly in light of everything that has happened," she said. "This charm represents forgiveness—something I think each one of you learned a great deal about this week."

Mom gave each one of us a charm that we added to our bracelets right away.

"Thanks, everybody!" Jenny said before we left. "I couldn't have a better group of friends!"

. . .

Later that night at home, Mom and Dad sat with Anna and me as we went to bed. I was super glad that God was right there with us. I was glad Anna was back from Grandma's house where she had stayed while we were gone. I said a prayer of thanks. I knew that I was very lucky to have such a great family and really terrific friends.

We gave each other a big hug. Then Mom read us a new poem that she'd written just for us.

I look upon your pretty face,
Filled with love and joy and grace.
You try so hard in all you do,
I'm so very proud of you.
You've grown in faith and learned a lot.
There's something special that you've got.
A quality that's oh so rare,
It shines through the ways you care.
Keep holding tight to God above
For you will find no greater love.

"**Hi!** Come be a part of the exciting adventures in our brand new DVD 'A Little Bit Of Faith'"

Feature Running Time: Approx. 30 minutes PLUS Bonus Features

Treasure
Your Charms!

The perfect place to keep your favorite bracelet, necklace and charms! Each time you open this musical jewelry box, Faith The Angel™ welcomes you with a smile!

Special Gift Set

The perfect gift for that special girl! Gift set includes: The First Chapter Book, Friendship Charm and Bracelet with Rainbow Charm. A $30 Value for only $19.95!

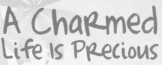

Up next for the Precious Girls Club: Book #7

Shining Through the Storm

Thunder exploded and streaks of light flashed through my room as Patches scooched farther under the covers. In the super dark a loud horn blared and my dad shouted, "Tornado siren! We have to get into the basement right now!"

I saw Faith's worried look as she pointed to the bedroom door. Then I felt my father's arms propel me forward quickly toward the basement door. My heart was beating faster than it had ever tried to beat before.

"Hurry, girls!" Mom said as she opened the door to the basement, shined her flashlight on the stairs, and led the way. Anna and I were right behind her.

"Aaaahhhh!" Anna screeched as she tumbled down several stairs. Mom tried to catch her, but they both toppled over and slowly bumped their way to the bottom. Our kitty, Sparky, escaped Anna's grasp, and dashed back up the steps. Daddy tried to help Mom and Anna up. I turned my head just in time to see Sparky scramble up the stairs, through the door, and out of sight.

I remembered my pledge to be the most caringest person in the Bennett family, and without thinking, I turned and ran up the stairs to get Sparky and bring her back down to the basement. Everyone yelled, "Katie, come back here!"

Then the house rattled in a way that I'd never experienced before. After that everything became a blur . . .

Read more in Shining Through the Storm in stores Spring 2010